CONTENTS

BUYING CANDIES

PART 1

"I get my allowance today,"

I told Leon at recess.

"Me too," said Leon.

"Let's go to the store this afternoon.

We'll buy some candies," I said.

We went to tell Marcos about it.

"Come to my house after school,"

I said.

When I went home

I got my allowance.

Then, Leon and Marcos arrived.

"We're going to buy some candies,"

I told my mom.

She handed me a letter.

"Would you please mail this

at the post office?" she asked.

"Don't forget!"

"I'll remember," I promised.

"What are you going to buy?"

I asked Leon and Marcos.

"I'm not sure yet," said Marcos.

"I want a chocolate bar," said Leon.

"I hear there are new candies

that look like little skulls.

I'm going to buy those," I said.

"Baba Yaga had skulls on the fence

around her house," said Marcos.

"Who is Baba Yaga?" I asked.

"I'll tell you a story about her,"

Marcos said.

★

BABA YAGA

(Marcos' Story)

Once there was a man and a woman

who had two children –

a girl and a boy.

One day, the parents

had to go to the market.

The mother said to the girl,

"Elena, while we're away,

take care of your baby brother.

But be careful!

The black geese of Baba Yaga

were seen flying over the village,

so don't go outside.

Now don't forget!

We'll bring you some sugar buns

when we come home."

Elena knew about Baba Yaga,

the terrible witch of the forest.

She was eight feet tall

and ate little children.

Elena stayed in the house

with her baby brother.

Very soon she got bored.

She saw her friends outside,

so she took her brother,

set him down on the grass,

and went to play with her friends.

She forgot all about him.

After some time, she remembered

and came back to look for him.

He was nowhere to be found.

Then, far away on the horizon,

Elena saw the black geese.

They were carrying something!

The geese had stolen her brother
and were taking him
to Baba Yaga's hut.
"I must go after him!"
Elena ran toward the forest
where Baba Yaga lived.
As she was running,
Elena came to a pond.
There, lying on the sand
was a fish, gasping for air.
"Please help me!" the fish called.
"I'm dying!"

Elena was in a hurry,

but she stopped and put the fish

back into the water.

The fish popped its head out.

"Because you helped me,

I will help you," it said.

"Pick up that shell by your feet.
If you're ever in danger,
throw it over your shoulder
and it will help you."
Elena picked up the shell
and put it in her pocket.

Then she ran on through the forest.

The trees grew so close together

that no light could shine

through them.

Finally, she came to a clearing . . .

and there was Baba Yaga's hut.

A skull fence stood around it,

and the black geese were sleeping

on the roof.

Elena climbed up to the hut

and peaked inside.

Baba Yaga was asleep, snoring.

Elena's brother was near her,

sitting on the ground,

playing with some bones.

Elena crept in,

grabbed her baby brother,

and ran outside.

But the black geese saw her.

"*HONK, HONK!*" they cried,

and flapped their wings.

They woke up Baba Yaga.

She ran out and screamed,

“STOP, THIEF!

Bring back my dinner!”

And she chased after them.

Elena ran as fast as she could,

but her brother was heavy.

Baba Yaga was getting

closer and closer.

When Elena looked back,

she saw Baba Yaga reach out.

What could she do?

She remembered the shell!

She threw it over her shoulder.

Instantly, a wide river appeared.

Baba Yaga could not go around it,

so she waded into it.

But the water was deep

and Baba Yaga couldn't swim.

In no time at all, she drowned.

Elena and her brother got home
just in time.
Then their parents returned
and gave them some sugar buns.

★ ★ ★

"What's a sugar bun?" Leon asked.

"I don't know.

A kind of doughnut, maybe,"

said Marcos.

"Why did Elena get doughnuts

even when she caused trouble?"

asked Leon.

"Well, luckily she was able
to make things right," I said.
"I know a story about a girl
who forgot something
and had no chance to fix it.
It's called *The Golden Arm*."

THE GOLDEN ARM

(My Story)

Once there were two sisters,

June and Edna.

June, the older one,

had a golden arm.

She was very proud of it

and liked it even better

than her real arm.

Every night June told Edna:

“If something happens

and I die,

don’t forget to bury me

with my golden arm.”

“I promise,” Edna told her.

When June was very old,

She got sick and died.

Edna buried her sister,

but forgot the golden arm.

It was left under the covers

in June's bed.

When Edna walked back
from the cemetery,
it started to snow and blow.
Edna got home, but felt so cold
that she crawled into June's bed
to warm herself up.

But she couldn't get warm,

because the golden arm was there

and it was as cold as ice.

Outside the wind squealed,

and Edna heard a voice moaning,

"W-h-e-e-r-e'-s my g-o-l-d-e-n

a-a-a-r-m?"

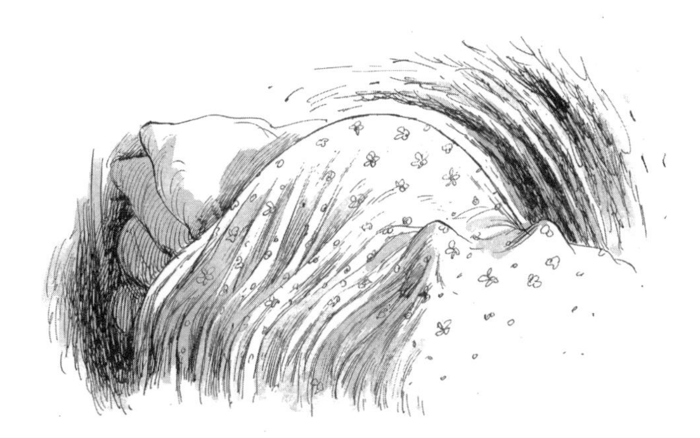

Edna pulled the covers

over her head.

But it was no use.

It came from the road:

"W-h-e-e-r-e'-s my . . ."

and from the porch:

" . . . g-o-l-d-e-n . . ."

and at the door:

" . . . a-a-a-r-m?"

And the voice and the wind

wailed under the door,

"W-H-E-E-R-E'-S MY

G-O-L-D-E-N A-A-A-R-M?"

Edna shivered.

Then she peeked out.

It was beside her.

And – it jumped. . . .

YOU'VE GOT IT!!!

★ ★ ★

"No, I don't!" cried Marcos.

"Leon has it!"

We chased after each other

and wrestled on the ground.

"I know a story about a boy

who forgot something too,"

said Leon.

"It's about a big, hairy monster."

"Well, tell us," I said.

"We're almost at the store."

MONSTER GOGO

(Leon's Story)

There was a woman

who had a son called Atu.

Their cottage was among fields

where no one else lived.

The woman kept four big dogs

to protect them, because at night

the hairy monster, Gogo,

wandered the countryside.

Gogo was always hungry.

He ate everything in sight –

animals or people –

they were all food to him.

Every day the woman cooked

a roast-beef dinner for the dogs.

And every evening she said,

“Keep watch through the night

in case Monster Gogo comes.”

The dogs would wag their tales

and say, “Sleep without fear.”

But one day, the woman

had to go to town.

"I will be back tomorrow,"

she told Atu.

"Roast the meat in the oven

and give the dogs their dinner.

Don't forget!"

When his mother left,

Atu put the meat in the oven.

Then the dogs began to bark.

Atu looked outside and saw

his friends were coming over.

“What’s that smell?

What’s cooking?” his friends asked.

“Can we a have a taste?”

“It’s for the dogs,” said Atu.

“*Woof, woof,*” said his friends,

pretending to be dogs.

They joked and laughed with Atu

and they ate all the meat.

Then they left to get home

before the sun went down

and Gogo came out.

The dogs came into the kitchen

looking for their dinner.

Atu put out the bowl

with a few scraps and a bone.

"Is that our dinner?" the dogs asked.

“Take it or leave it,” said Atu.

“I’m tired. I’m going to bed.”

“It seems we must get our dinner

somewhere else,” the dogs said.

They ran far across the fields

all the way to the next farm.

Atu went to sleep.

But what was that sound outside?

PLOP. PLOP. Heavy feet

pounded the garden path.

Monster Gogo!

Atu locked the door

and went to bed.

CRASH! The door banged open.

CLING, CLANG! The dishes fell.

Atu opened the attic door

and climbed up into it.

Soon Gogo poked his head

through the opening.

Atu opened the attic window,

climbed down to the ground,

hid in a big clay pot,

and pulled the lid on tight.

SNIFF, SNIFF, Gogo came around

smelling the pot. . . .

★ ★ ★

BUYING CANDIES
PART 2

We came to the store.

"Can I finish my story later?"

asked Leon.

"I need chocolate – right now."

We went in and looked around.

"Do you have the candies

that look like small skulls?"

I asked the lady in the store.

"No," she said. "We're sold out.

We'll have more next week."

So, I chose candies

that looked like purple snakes.

Leon picked a chocolate bar,

and Marcos bought gum.

"Anything else?" asked the lady.

"That will be all," we said,

and we gave her our money.

Outside, we ate all our treats.

"Let's play ball at my house,"

I said to Leon and Marcos.

We ran back home.

My mom came outside and asked,

"Did you mail my letter?"

"Letter?"

I looked. The letter was still

in my pocket.

"Oh, no! I forgot!

I will go back," I offered.

"It's too late," said my mother.

"The post office is closed now.

You were supposed to help!

I'll do it myself tomorrow."

My mom was in a bad mood.

"I think we better go now,"

said Leon and Marcos,

and suddenly, they were gone.

But, I thought, *we said*

we would play ball!

How could *they forget?*

AFTERWORD

The boys were so greedy for candy

that they forgot something else!

Leon never finished his story.

It's up to you to think up

an ending for *Monster Gogo*.

How will Atu escape? Or will he?

WHERE THE STORIES COME FROM

There are folktales from many lands

about someone who has trouble

because he or she forgets

to do something.

Baba Yaga is a Russian story.

The Golden Arm comes from England.

Monster Gogo is based on

part of a tale from West Africa.